No Puppies Today!

by Joanna Cole
Illustrated by Brian Karas

ScottForesman

A Division of HarperCollinsPublishers

I wanted a puppy, so I went to Mr. Potter's Pet Shop. Mr. Potter looked all around but he couldn't find a puppy.

"No puppies today!" he said.

"Try this pet."

So I went home with

ONE huge gray elephant.

My mother said, "No!"

So I went back to

Mr. Potter's Pet Shop.

"I can't have an elephant," I said.

"I want a puppy!"

Mr. Potter looked up and down,

but he didn't see any puppies.

"Try these pets," he said.

"They are better than a puppy."

So I went home with

TWO tall giraffes.

My mother and my father said,

"No, no, no!"

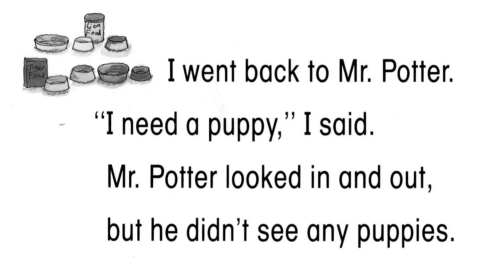 I went back to Mr. Potter.

"I need a puppy," I said.

Mr. Potter looked in and out,

but he didn't see any puppies.

"These pets need a loving home!"
he said.

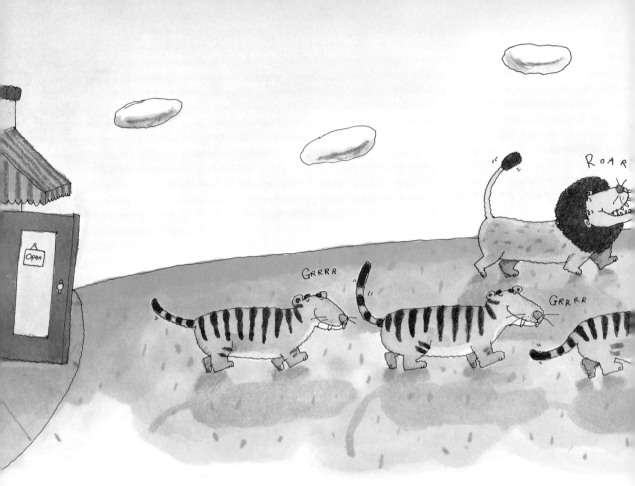

So I went home with
THREE roaring lions and
FOUR growling tigers.

My mother and my father
and my sister said,
"Help, help, help!"

13

"No lions or tigers," I told Mr. Potter.

Mr. Potter looked under and over,

and he gave me FIVE brown bison.

My mother and my father and
my sister and my brother said,
"Take them back!"

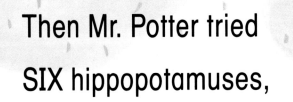

Then Mr. Potter tried

SIX hippopotamuses,

SEVEN rhinoceroses,

EIGHT yellow monkeys,

NINE jumping kangaroos,

and TEN pink flamingos.

My mother and my father

and my sister and my brother

and my grandma and my grandpa

and my aunt and my uncle

and my cousins and my neighbors

all shouted,

"GET THEM OUT OF HERE!"

Then Mr. Potter
looked all around . . .
and up and down . . .
and in and out . . .
and over and under . . .

and look what he found!

A puppy for me!